The Upstairs Downstairs Bears on Holiday

by Carol Lawson

For

Amy, Charis, David, George, Holly and James

First published in Great Britain 1997
by Heinemann Young Books
Published 1998 by Mammoth
an imprint of Reed International Books Limited
Michelin House, 81 Fulham Road, London SW3 6RB
10 9 8 7 6 5 4 3 2 1

Text and illustrations copyright © Carol Lawson 1997
Carol Lawson has asserted her moral rights.

0 7497 3424 8

A CIP catalogue record for this title
is available from the British Library

Printed in the UAE by Oriental Press Ltd.

Freddy

Henry

Alice

Henrietta

Baby Arthur

Barker

Number 49
Theodore Square

Kitty

Winston

Flora Mardle

Mrs Bumble

Polly

Nanny Maybold

It was seven o'clock in the morning and Henry and Alice Bosworth were already wide awake, excitedly packing their favourite toys. Today was the first day of the summer holidays and the Bosworth family were leaving 49, Theodore Square for Blossom Melbury and their house in the country.

In the nursery, Nanny Maybold was dressing Baby Arthur.

Down the passage, doing her best not to wake Mr and Mrs Bosworth, Flora was folding dresses and shirts in tissue paper and placing them carefully in the big canvas trunk.

Meanwhile, in the kitchen, Mrs Bumble was packing a hamper of food for supper that night and a little something for a picnic along the way.

Barker supervised all the travelling arrangements: Henry and Alice were going to travel with Papa and Mama and Flora and Winston in Papa's motor car. Kitty was to go by train with Polly, Nanny Maybold and Baby Arthur. The other Downstairs Bears would close up the house and follow on the next day.

As soon as breakfast was over, Winston brought the car round to the front door. Everybody climbed in and Freddy Bosworth took the wheel.

"Don't forget your hamper," said Mrs Bumble. "It's under the seat."

"And remember, twins," called Nanny Maybold, "a polite bear is a welcome bear!"

Poop! Poop! As Freddy drove slowly out of the square, a taxi cab passed him on the way to number 49.

"All aboard for Paddington station!" called the driver.

Freddy Bosworth was enjoying himself.

"Careful, Mr Frederick!" said Winston as Freddy speeded along. "We've a lot of luggage on board."

"Goodness!" shouted Henrietta, "do watch out, Freddy!"

Freddy tried to brake but the car lurched out of control and the bears found themselves rattling down a bumpy lane that ended in a shallow stream.

The engine spluttered, sighed and was silent.

"Splendid spot for a picnic, don't you think?" said Freddy,
pulling off his goggles. "Help me down with the hamper,
Winston old chap."

After lunch, while Freddy and Henrietta dozed in the sun,
Flora and Winston took the twins down to the stream for
a paddle. Flora showed them how to make paper boats and
they played until it was time to set off again.

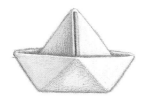 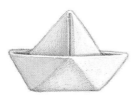 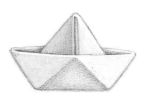

"Melbury Junction!" called out Mr Honeywig, the station master, as the London train steamed to a halt.

Kitty had already pulled down the window to look at the people waiting on the platform. "Where's Binkie?" she cried. "He promised to meet us."

"Quick, Miss Kitty, open the door," said Nanny Maybold, getting flustered. "All eyes and no action will get us nowhere."

The little group stood surrounded by luggage, and Baby Arthur began to cry, when suddenly they heard *ting-a-ling* and a small bear on a huge Penny Farthing came wobbling down the platform towards them.

"Kitty, sweetheart, it's me, Binkie! Welcome to Blossom Melbury! Oh, oh, I can't stop . . ."

Kitty watched open-mouthed as Binkie careered past them, past the ticket collector and out of the station. They heard him call faintly, "Follow me! Farmer Brewin's waiting."

It was well after six when everyone finally gathered on the lawn for a glass of Mrs Bumble's homemade lemonade.

"As a special treat we'll eat in the garden this evening," announced Henrietta.

Flora went to fetch the pie that Mrs Bumble had packed for their supper but she returned looking puzzled.

"Excuse me, Madam, but the hamper seems to be empty."

Henrietta looked accusingly at Freddy and there was a gloomy silence. Then Binkie jumped up. "Come on, Freddy," he said. "We're going fishing!"

The moon was up by the time the fishing party returned from their expedition. The bears gathered happily under the walnut tree to eat salmon and potatoes cooked on an open fire. Delicious!

"Up the wooden hill to Bedfordshire! There's another day tomorrow," said Nanny Maybold.

"It's not fair," complained Alice. "Why do we have to go to bed when everyone else is having fun?"

"Let's see what they're doing," said Henry. The two little bears crept out of bed and clambered up onto the window seat.

"Look at Binkie," said Henry, pointing to a shadowy figure in the rhododendrons. "Whatever is he doing?"

"He's serenading Kitty with his banjo!" squeaked Alice.

Having swept and polished and drawn the curtains at 49, Theodore Square, Mrs Bumble covered the furniture with white sheets. Barker checked that everything was in order, then they locked up the house and set off for the station and Blossom Melbury.

Farmer Brewin met them in his trap. "It's the Regatta on Melbury Lake this afternoon," he said as he took their cases. "Would you like to be my crew, Mrs Bumble?"

Mrs Bumble giggled. "Very kind, I'm sure," she said, "but my place is on the bank with Nanny Maybold and the little ones."

Down by the lake everyone was waiting for the big race to begin. "Twice round Pirate Island, double back past Rocky Green and the first bear home is the winner!" shouted Parson Beaney. "Come on, Papa!" cheered the little bears.

"Come on, Binkie!" cried Kitty. "You can do it!"

"Well begun is half done!" said Nanny Maybold as the flotilla of little boats began to jostle for position.

Alice and Henry soon got bored with watching the boats so
Flora gave them some paper and pencils to keep them quiet.

When the race was over, the Blossom Melbury cup was presented to Binkie. "My hero!" sighed Kitty. Then there were more speeches.

"Come on, Alice," whispered Henry, "follow me."

"Nanny said we mustn't go near the water," said Alice.

"We won't," said Henry. "We'll just sit in Binkie's boat and play at being pirates."

The twins clambered aboard and soon, lulled by the rocking of the waves, they fell fast asleep.

Scrunch-bump went the boat against the jetty and *creak* went the rope that secured the *Pretty Kitty*. The twins awoke to find themselves stranded on a rocky shore.

"Henry!" exclaimed Alice, "we're shipwrecked."

"Don't panic," said Henry. "I can see Melbury harbour."

"But Henry, that means we're on the island - Pirate Island!"

"We're not scared, are we?" said Henry nervously.

"Of course not," said Alice hurriedly. "Let's explore."

Nanny Maybold looked around for the twins. Seeing no sign of them, and feeling slightly anxious, she ran to the jetty.

The first drops of rain were beginning to fall when she collided with Binkie.

"My boat!" he exclaimed. "It's disappeared."

"Oh my!" cried Nanny Maybold, "and so have the twins!"

By this time everyone had gathered on the jetty. "We'll take my boat and search the lake," said Freddy.

"My poor babies!" cried Henrietta. "You must go at once!"

Over on Pirate Island, the twins looked up at the dark sky and shivered in the cold gusts of wind.

"I don't want to play pirates any more," said Henry. "I want to go home."

Just then they saw Papa's boat passing the island. They waved and shouted but no one saw them.

"We'll have to send a message so that they know where we are," said Alice. "I know, I've got an idea!"

It was Binkie who saw the flash of white on the dark waves.
"Why, it's one of the twin's paper boats!" Freddy shouted as
he fished it out of the water. "And look, it's made out of a
Jolly Roger. That must be a clue to show where they are."
He thought hard for a moment, then . . ."Got it!" he cried.
"Steer a course for Pirate Island, Binkie old chum!" Swiftly
they turned and headed back towards the island.

Soon two bedraggled little teddies were being lifted into the *Saucy Susan*. All the bears on the jetty cheered when they saw that they were safe.

"Those naughty twins! They promised they wouldn't go near the water. They will be put to bed straight away when we get home," said Nanny Maybold sternly. "Once they are warm and dry and have had a hot drink, that is . . ."

The storm blew itself out overnight, and the next morning dawned bright and sunny. Farmer Brewin, however, was worried that the weather might break again so all the bears set off to help him bring in the harvest.

It was hard work gathering up the golden corn but everyone
joined in while Barker kept an eye on things. At midday, Flora
and Polly brought lunch and cool lemonade to the thirsty
workers.

Suddenly there was a rumble. "Is that thunder?" said Farmer Brewin, peering around anxiously.

"Is that a rain cloud?" said his daughter Molly pointing at a large dark cloud that had appeared in the sky.

"It's Binkie!" shouted the twins.

"I've come to help," he cried over the noise of the steam engine. "Oh, oh, I can't stop . . ."

By dusk, the work was finished and all the corn was neatly stooked.

"Now, to thank you for your help," said Farmer Brewin, "you are all invited to come back to the barn for our Harvest Celebrations!"

It was nearly midnight and the harvest moon was shining brightly by the time the party was over.

"I wish we could stay in Blossom Melbury forever," said Alice, tugging on Flora's apron as they headed for home.

Flora smiled. "Well, I expect we will all be back next summer, and every summer after that, so it's almost like forever, isn't it?"

Freddy, carrying a sleepy Henry on his shoulders, led the tired but happy bears down the lane, while Kitty and Binkie lingered behind, savouring the scent of wild roses that wafted from the hedgerows.